Speak your mind even if your voice shakes.
— Maggie Kuhn

voice becomes powerful."
Malala Yousafzai

Use your voice for kindness, your ears for compassion, your hands for charity, your mind for truth, and your Heart for Love.

"I stand for honesty, equality, kindness, compassion treating people the way you'd want to be treated and helping those in need.

To me, those are traditional values. That's what I stand for.

I also believe in dance."

LITTLE GIRLS WITH DREAMS BECOME WOMEN WITH VISION.
—UNKNOWN

"
Leadership is not bullying and leadership is not aggression. Leadership is the expectation that you can use your voice for good. That you can make the world a better place.

WELL BEHAVED WOMEN RARELY MAKE HISTORY
—ELEANOR ROOSEVELT

SHE BELIEVED SHE COULD SO SHE DID
—R S GREY

For every girl.

This book was inspired by the story of the first female U.S. Olympian boxer, Claressa Shields.

ISBN# 978-0-578-46302-5

I'm a GIRL Hear MY ROAR

Written, illustrated, designed & published by

SARAH LAROSE KANE

Your **ROAR** is your **voice.**

You need to use it so you have a choice.

a CHOICe
to be free!

A **ROAR** is **STRONG**, it is **BRAVE**, and it is **LOUD.**

Like the **ROAR**
of a lion,

it is

PROUD.

I'm a GIRL
HEAR MY ROAR!
I have BIG dreams
and I will SOAR!

I am BRAVE,
I am PROUD
and I am SMART
and though I am strong,
I have a big HEART.

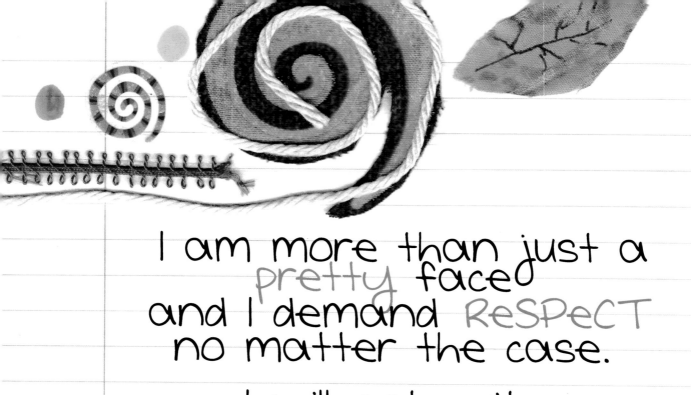

I am more than just a
pretty face
and I demand ReSPeCT
no matter the case.

I will not quit
and I will fight
to stand up for
what is right!

I am kind
but that doesn't make me weak.
SO LiSTeN UP, NoW,
WHeN I SPeAK!!

Shwew!

That was GREAT girls!!
Doesn't it feel GOOD,

to speak your voice
so you're understood?

This idea did not come from me!

Margaret Fuller
(1810-1850)

Susan B Anthony
(1820-1906)

Sappho
(570 BC)

Joan of Arc
(1412-1431)

Sojourner Truth
(1797-1883)

Millicent Fawcett
(1846-1929)

Helen Keller
(1880-1968)

Cleopatra
(69BC-30BC)

Eleanor of Aquitaine
(1122-1204)

Elizabeth Cady Stanton
(1815-1902)

Harriet
Beecher Stowe
(1811-1896)

Cocoa Chanel
(1883-1971)

Hildegard of Bingen
(1098-1179)

Florence
Nightingale
(1820-1910)

It's been passed down through women in history!

Rosa Parks
(1913-2005)

Betty Friedan
(1921-2006)

Billie Jean King
(1943-)

Margaret Thatcher

(1925-2013)

Mother Teresa
(1910-1997)

Billie Holiday
(1915-1959)

Audrey Hepburn
(1929-1993)

Malala Yousafzai
(1997-)

Dorothy Hodgkin
(1910-1994)

Anne Frank
(1929-1945)

Betty Williams
(1943-)

Tegla Loroupe
(1973-)

Eleanor Roosevelt
(1884-1962)

Benazir Bhutto
(1953-2007)

J.K. Rowling
(1965-)

They used their voices
to bring us victories

over many different
inequalities.

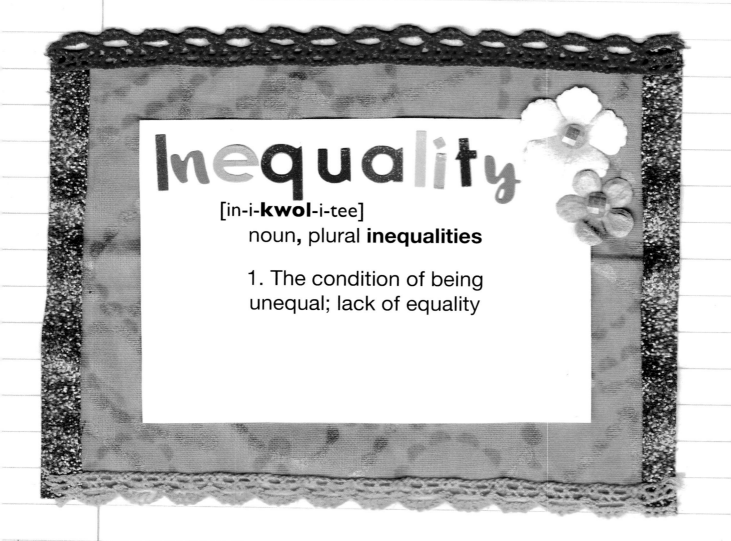

Inequality

[in-i-**kwol**-i-tee]
noun, plural **inequalities**

1. The condition of being
unequal; lack of equality

WOMEN
bring all
VOTERS
into the world
~
Let Women Vote

EQUAL PAY
- NOW!

EQUAL PAY Day MARCH

EQUAL PAY Day MARCH

RIGHT TO EDUCATION

EQUAL OPPORTUNITIES FOR WORK AND EDUCATION

WE DEMAND THE RIGHT TO WORK

WOMEN WORKERS ARE BEING TAKEN FOR A RIDE

WE MARCH FOR INTEGRATED SCHOOLS NOW!

WE DEMAND EQUAL RIGHTS NOW!

WE DEMAND DECENT HOUSING NOW!

WE DEMAND AN END TO BIAS NOW!

Equal Rights

WOMEN for CONGRESS
THE WOMAN'S PARTY CANDIDATES

They overcame things
people said they couldn't.
They even did things
people said they shouldn't.

Kathrine Switzer-

Ran the Boston marathon after she was told she couldn't.

Billie Jean King-
Professional tennis player who beat a man at her sport when no one said she could.

Sirimavo Bandaranaike-
The world's very first female leader of a country.

Rosa Parks-
Sat in the front of the bus when she was told she couldn't.

Valentina Tereshkova-
First female in outer space.

Amelia Earhart- First woman to fly solo across the Atlantic Ocean.

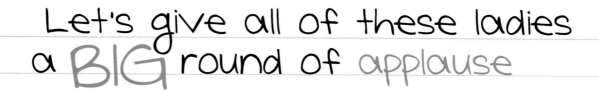

Let's give all of these ladies
a **BIG** round of applause

for making a change
and fighting for our cause!

We learn from them
and with a grateful heart

we carry the torch
to do our part.

confidence Integrity
Strength
determination

Bravery
Pride
Vision
courage

The world needs

YOU

and needs your

VOICE in it.

This I promise you,
so don't you ever forget it.

So, I have just one question for you today...
What is YOUR
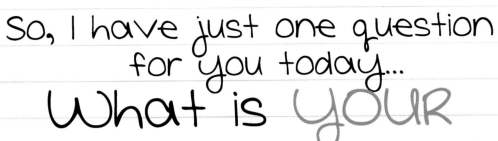
ROAR

and what does it say?!

My ROAR:

The End
(of inequality)

A NOTE FROM THE ARTHUR

GIRLS!

The torch has been passed to you!

Write your own roar in your book where it says, "My ROAR:"

Before you write it, I want you to think about what you want the world to know about you. What do you dream of becoming? What are your strengths? What words will you use to stand up for yourself? How are you going to make the world a better place?

Once you've written it, practice saying it out loud—with confidence! Your voice is like a muscle. The more you use it, the stronger it gets. We can't keep our roars to ourselves! The world needs to hear it! So, I want you to rap it, sing it, recite it or write it and get it on social media (with permission!) Hashtag your post, #imagirlhearmyroar, or go to the Facebook page, I'm a Girl Hear my Roar, and submit it there. Let's create a movement, cheer each other on and be heard!!

Most importantly, if you have been holding in a serious secret or feel like you've been treated in a way that isn't right, be brave, and use your voice to tell an adult that you trust.

ROAR!

Sarah LaRose Kane

Cleopatra (69-30 BCE)

The last Ptolemaic ruler of Egypt. Cleopatra sought to defend Egypt from the expanding Roman Empire. In doing so she formed relationships with two of Rome's most powerful leaders, Marc Anthony and Julius Caesar. She was known for her intellect and spoke 9 different languages.

Sappho (570 BC)

One of the first known female writers. Much of her poetry has been lost, but her immense reputation has remained. Plato referred to Sappho as one of the 10 great poets.

Hildegard of Bingen (1098-1179)

Mystic, author and composer. Hildegard of Bingen lived a withdrawn life, spending most of her time behind convent walls. However, her writings, poetry and music were revelatory for the time period. She was consulted by popes, kings and influential people of the time. Her writings and music have influenced people to this day.

Eleanor of Aquitaine (1122-1204)

First Queen of France. Eleanor was one of the wealthiest and most powerful figures in Europe during the middle ages. She maintained control over her life in a time when women yielded power to their husbands.

Joan of Arc (1412-1431)

The patron saint of France. At the age of 17, Joan disguised herself as a man and lead France to Victory over England.

Sojourner Truth (1797-1883)

African-American abolitionist and women's rights campaigner. In 1851, she gave a famous extemporaneous speech, "Ain't I a woman?" which explained in plain language how women were equal to men.

Margaret Fuller (1810–1850)–

An American women's rights advocate. Her book *Women in the Nineteenth Century* (1845) was influential in changing perceptions about men and women, and was one of the most important early feminist works. She argued for equality and women being more self-dependent and less dependent on men.

Harriet Beecher Stowe (1811–1896)

A lifelong anti-slavery campaigner. Her novel *Uncle Tom's Cabin* was a bestseller and helped to popularize the anti-slavery campaign. Abraham Lincoln later remarked that her books were a major factor behind the American civil war.

Elizabeth Cady Stanton (1815–1902)

American social activist and leading figure in the early women's rights movement. She was a key figure in helping create the early women's suffrage movements in the US.

Susan B Anthony (1820–1906)

American Campaigner against slavery and for the promotion of women's and workers rights. She began campaigning within the temperance movement, and this convinced her of the necessity for women to have the vote. She toured the US giving countless speeches on the subjects of human rights.

Helen Keller (1880–1968)

(1880–1968) American social activist. At the age of 19 months, Helen became deaf and blind. Overcoming the frustration of losing both sight and hearing, she campaigned tirelessly on behalf of deaf and blind people.

Florence Nightingale (1820–1906)

British nurse. By serving in the Crimean war, Florence Nightingale was instrumental in changing the role and perception of the nursing profession. Her dedicated service won widespread admiration and led to a significant improvement in the treatment of wounded soldiers.

Millicent Fawcett (1846-1929)

A leading suffragist and campaigner for equal rights for women. She led Britain's biggest suffrage organization, the non-violent (NUWSS) and played a key role in gaining women the vote. She also helped found Newnham College, Cambridge.

Coco Chanel (1883-1971)

French fashion designer. One of the most innovative fashion designers, Coco Chanel was instrumental in defining feminine style and dress during the 20th Century. Her ideas were revolutionary; in particular she often took traditionally male clothes and redesigned them for the benefit of women.

Mother Teresa (1910-1997)

Albanian nun and charity worker. Devoting her life to the service of the poor and dispossessed, Mother Teresa became a global icon for selfless service to others. Through her Missionary of Charities organization, she personally cared for thousands of sick and dying people in Calcutta. She was awarded the Nobel Peace prize in 1979.

Dorothy Hodgkin (1910-1944)

British chemist. Awarded the Nobel prize for her work on critical discoveries of the structure of both penicillin and later insulin. These discoveries led to significant improvements in health care. An outstanding chemist, Dorothy also devoted a large section of her life to the peace movement and promoting nuclear disarmament.

Eleanor Roosevelt (1884-1962)

Wife and political aide of American president F.D.Roosevelt. In her own right, Eleanor made a significant contribution to the field of human rights, a topic she campaigned upon throughout her life. As head of UN human rights commission, she helped to draft the 1948 UN declaration of human rights.

Billie Holiday (1915-1959)

American jazz singer. Given the title "First Lady of the Blues," Billie Holiday was widely considered to be the greatest and most expressive jazz singer of all time. Her voice was moving in its emotional intensity and poignancy. Despite dying at the age of only 44, Billie Holiday helped define the jazz era and her recordings are still widely sold today.

Betty Friedan (1921-2006)

American social activist and leading feminist figure of the 1960s. She wrote the best-selling book "The Feminine Mystique." Friedan campaigned for an extension of female rights and an end to sexual discrimination.

Anne Frank (1929-1945)

Dutch Jewish author. Anne Frank's diary is one of the most widely read books in the world. It reveals the thoughts of a young, yet surprisingly mature 13-year-old girl, confined to a secret hiding place. "Despite everything, I believe that people are really good at heart."

Audrey Hepburn (1929-1993)

British actress. An influential female actor of the 1950s and 60s, Audrey Hepburn defined feminine glamour and dignity, and was later voted as one of the most beautiful women of the twentieth century. After her acting career ended in the mid 1960s, she devoted the remaining period of her life to humanitarian work with UNICEF.

Rosa Parks (1913-2005)

American civil rights activist. Rosa Parks' refusal to give up her bus seat in Montgomery, Alabama, indirectly led to some of the most significant civil rights legislation of American history. She sought to play down her role in the civil rights struggle, but for her peaceful and dignified campaigning, she became one of the most well respected figures in the civil rights movements.

Billie Jean King (1947-)

American tennis player. Billie Jean King was one of the greatest female tennis champions, who also battled for equal pay for women. She won 67 professional titles including 20 titles at Wimbledon.

Betty Williams (1943-)

Together with Mairead Corrigan, Betty Williams campaigned to bring an end to the sectarian violence in Northern Ireland. They founded the Community for Peace and were awarded the Nobel Peace Prize in 1977 (post dated for 1976).

Benazir Bhutto (1953-2007)

The first female prime minister of a Muslim country. She helped to move Pakistan from a dictatorship to democracy, becoming Prime Minister in 1988. She sought to implement social reforms, in particular helping women and the poor. She was assassinated in 2007.

Margaret Thatcher (1925-2013)

The first female Prime minister of Great Britain, she governed for over 10 years, putting emphasis on individual responsibility and a belief in free markets.

Tegla Loroupe (1973-)

Kenyan athlete. Loroupe held the women's marathon world record and won many prestigious marathons. Since retiring from running, she has devoted herself to various initiatives promoting peace, education and women's rights. In her native Kenya, her Peace Race and Peace Foundation have been widely praised for helping to end tribal conflict.

J.K. Rowling (1965-)

British author of the phenomenal best selling Harry Potter series. The volume of sales was so high, it has been credited with leading a revival of reading by children. She wrote the first book as a single mother, struggling to make ends meet, but her writing led to her great success.

Malala Yousafzai (1997-)

Pakistani schoolgirl who defied threats of the Taliban to campaign for the right to education. She survived being shot in the head by the Taliban and has become a global advocate for women's rights, especially the right to education.

Your photo

MEET THE ARTHUR

It's a family joke of Sarah's, that she is an "Arthur," rather than an author—After her first publication in 2016, her 6 year old son (excitedly jumping up and down) told everyone he saw that, "My mom is an Arthur!!"
So, the endearing title stuck.

Sarah LaRose Kane is a fine artist, illustrator and author out of Kansas City, MO. She lives there with her husband, two boys and giant cat.

To learn more about Sarah and to see her other books and works of art, visit sarahlarosekane.com.

Thank you **to my husband and sons, for being such gentlemen and for your constant love, encouragement and support.** *Thank you* **to my sisters and mom for reminding me of the importance of writing this book when I was mentally or physically exhausted.**

Thank you **to my very affordable editor and friend, Penny Batt.** *Thank you* **to my son, Cruz, for letting me use the Crayola markers Santa brought him for Christmas.** *Thank you* **to biographyonline.net for the biographies on these amazing women in our history.** *Thank you* **to ESPN for highlighting female athletes, like Claressa Shields. Your story on Claressa was my inspiration for writing this book.** *Thank you* **to Create Space for providing the vehicle I needed to use my voice.**

Finally, an emphatic *thank you* **to all of the women who have blazed the trail and helped change the course of history. I wish I could fit you all in this book!**